Mr. Gumpy's Motor Car

John Burningham

Thomas Y. Crowell Company · New York

JE

Other books by John Burningham
BORKA
TRUBLOFF
ABC
HUMBERT
CANNONBALL SIMP
HARQUIN
SEASONS
MR. GUMPY'S OUTING
AROUND THE WORLD IN EIGHTY DAYS
LITTLE BOOKS: THE BABY, THE SCHOOL, THE RABBIT, THE SNOW

Friezes by John Burningham
BIRDLAND
LIONLAND
STORYLAND
JUNGLELAND
WONDERLAND
AROUND THE WORLD FRIEZE

Copyright©1973 by John Burningham. All rights reserved. First United States Publication 1976.
Typography and title-page design by Jan Pienkowski. Printed in the U.S.A.

Library of Congress Cataloging in Publication Data
Burningham, John. Mr. Gumpy's motor car.
SUMMARY: Mr. Gumpy's human and animal friends squash
into his old car and go for a drive—until it starts to rain.
(1. Automobile driving—Fiction) I.Title.
PZ7.B936Mg   (E)   75-4582
ISBN 0-690-00798-1   ISBN 0-690-00799-X (CQR)

Mr. Gumpy was going for a ride in his car.

He drove out of the gate and down the lane.

"May we come too?" said the children.

"May we?" said the rabbit, the cat, the dog, the pig, the sheep, the chickens, the calf, and the goat.

"All right," said Mr. Gumpy.
"But it will be a squash."

And they all piled in.

"It's a lovely day," said Mr. Gumpy. "Let's take the old dirt road across the fields."

For a while they drove along happily. The sun shone, the engine chugged, and everyone was enjoying the ride.

"I don't like the look of those clouds. I think it's going to rain," said Mr. Gumpy.

Very soon the dark clouds were right overhead. Mr. Gumpy stopped the car. He jumped out, put up the top, and down came the rain.

The road grew muddier and muddier,
and the wheels began to spin.
Mr. Gumpy looked at the hill ahead.

"Some of you will have to get out and push,"
he said.

"Not me," said the goat. "I'm too old."

"Not me," said the calf. "I'm too young."

"Not us," said the chickens. "We can't push."

"Not me," said the sheep. "I might catch cold."

"Not me," said the pig.
          "I've a bone in my trotter."

"Not me," said the dog.
          "But I'll drive if you like."

"Not me," said the cat. "It would ruin my fur."

"Not me," said the rabbit. "I'm not very well."

"Not me," said the girl. "He's stronger."

"Not me," said the boy. "She's bigger."

The wheels churned....

The car sank deeper into the mud.
"Now we're really stuck," said Mr. Gumpy.
They all got out and pushed.

They pushed and shoved and heaved and strained and gasped and slipped and slithered and squelched.

Slowly the car began to move....

"Don't stop!" cried Mr. Gumpy. "Keep it up! We're nearly there."

Everyone gave a mighty heave — the tires gripped....

The car edged its way to the top of the hill.
They looked up and saw that the sun
was shining again.
It began to get hot.

"We'll drive home across the bridge,"
said Mr. Gumpy.
"Then you can go for a swim."

And they did.
After a while it was time to go home.

"Good-bye," said Mr. Gumpy.
"Come for a drive another day."